D1237748

First published in Switzerland under the title *Geschichte ohne Ende und Anfang*.

First published in the United States, Great Britain, Canada, Australia, and New Zealand in 2009
by North-South Books Inc., an imprint of NordSüd Verlag AG, Zürich, Switzerland.
Distributed in the United States by North-South Books Inc., New York.

Library of Congress Cataloging-in-Publication Data is available.
ISBN: 978-0-7358-2203-0 (trade edition).
2 4 6 8 10 9 7 5 3 1
Printed in Belgium

www.northsouth.com

LITTLE ANT BIG THINKER

OR

Where does the Ocean End?

BY ANDRE USATSCHOW

ILLUSTRATED BY ALEXANDRA JUNGE

NorthSouth

NEW YORK / LONDON

One day a little ant stood at the edge of the ocean. So much water! So many waves!

"The ocean is big," he thought. "Do the waves roll on forever?"

"Does the ocean never end?" wondered the little ant. "If only I could see the other side."

He was a very little ant. But he was a very big thinker.

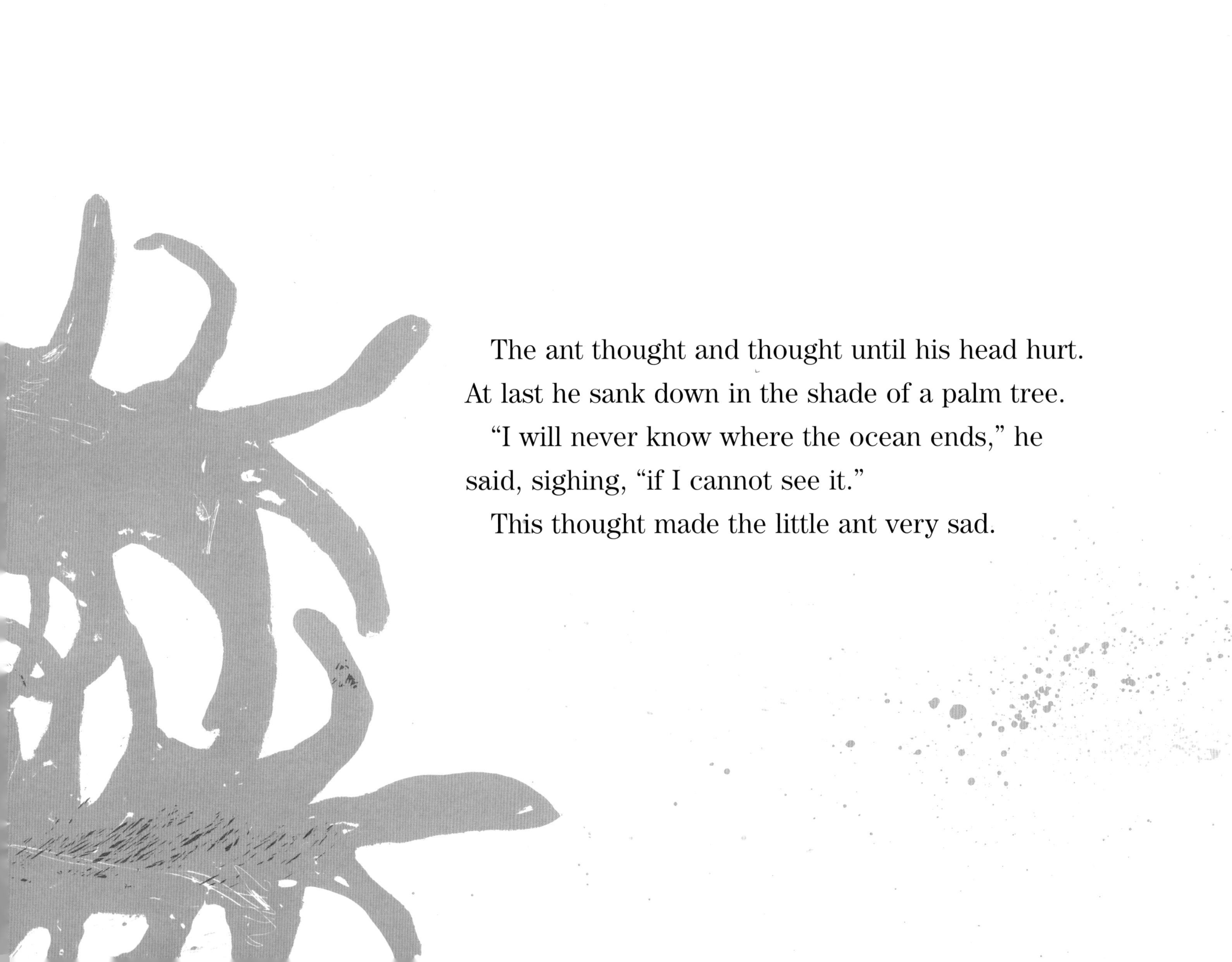

The ant thought and thought until his head hurt. At last he sank down in the shade of a palm tree.

"I will never know where the ocean ends," he said, sighing, "if I cannot see it."

This thought made the little ant very sad.

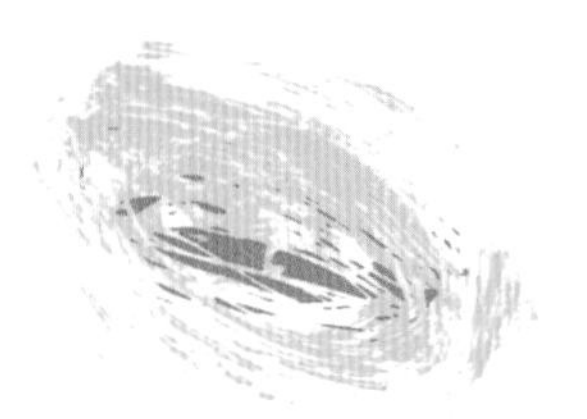

“What’s wrong?” said a voice. An elephant was looking down at him.

“I cannot see where the ocean ends.” The ant sniffed. “This is something I will never know.”

“That is sad,” said the elephant. “Maybe if we stood on tiptoe . . .”

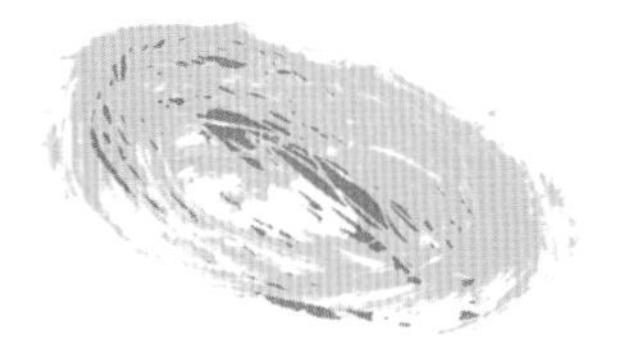

So the ant and the elephant stood on tiptoe.
“I see a small boat,” said the elephant.
“Do you see the end of the ocean?” asked the ant.
“I’m afraid not,” said the elephant.
“Neither do I,” said the ant.

Now they were both feeling so sad that they flopped down in the sand and cried.

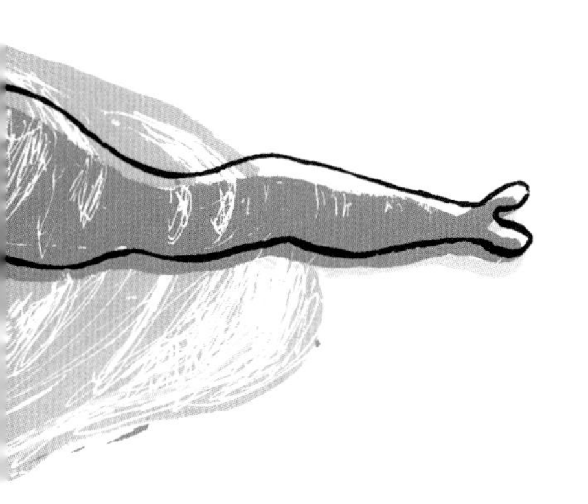

Suddenly the little ant sprang to his feet.

"I have an idea!" he cried. "We need to climb higher."

"Good thinking," said the elephant.

So the ant climbed onto the elephant, and the elephant climbed up the palm tree. But still all they saw was ocean and ocean and more ocean.

Then along came a big fish.

"What are you crying about up in that tree?" the fish called to the ant and the elephant.

"We're looking for the end of the ocean," said the ant, "but we can't see it."

"Is that all?" said the fish. "I've been swimming for a long, long time. And I can tell you, the ocean ends right here."

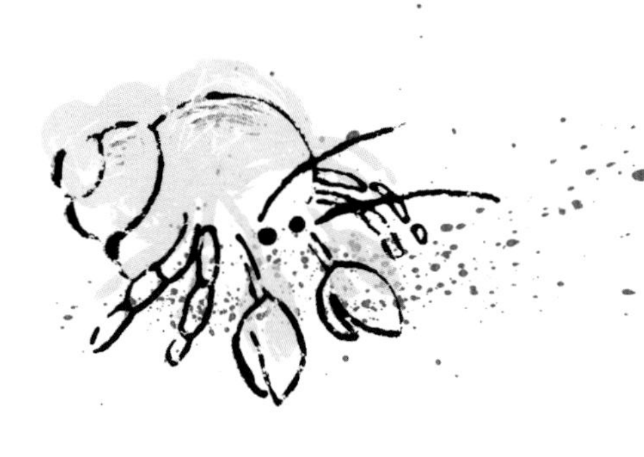

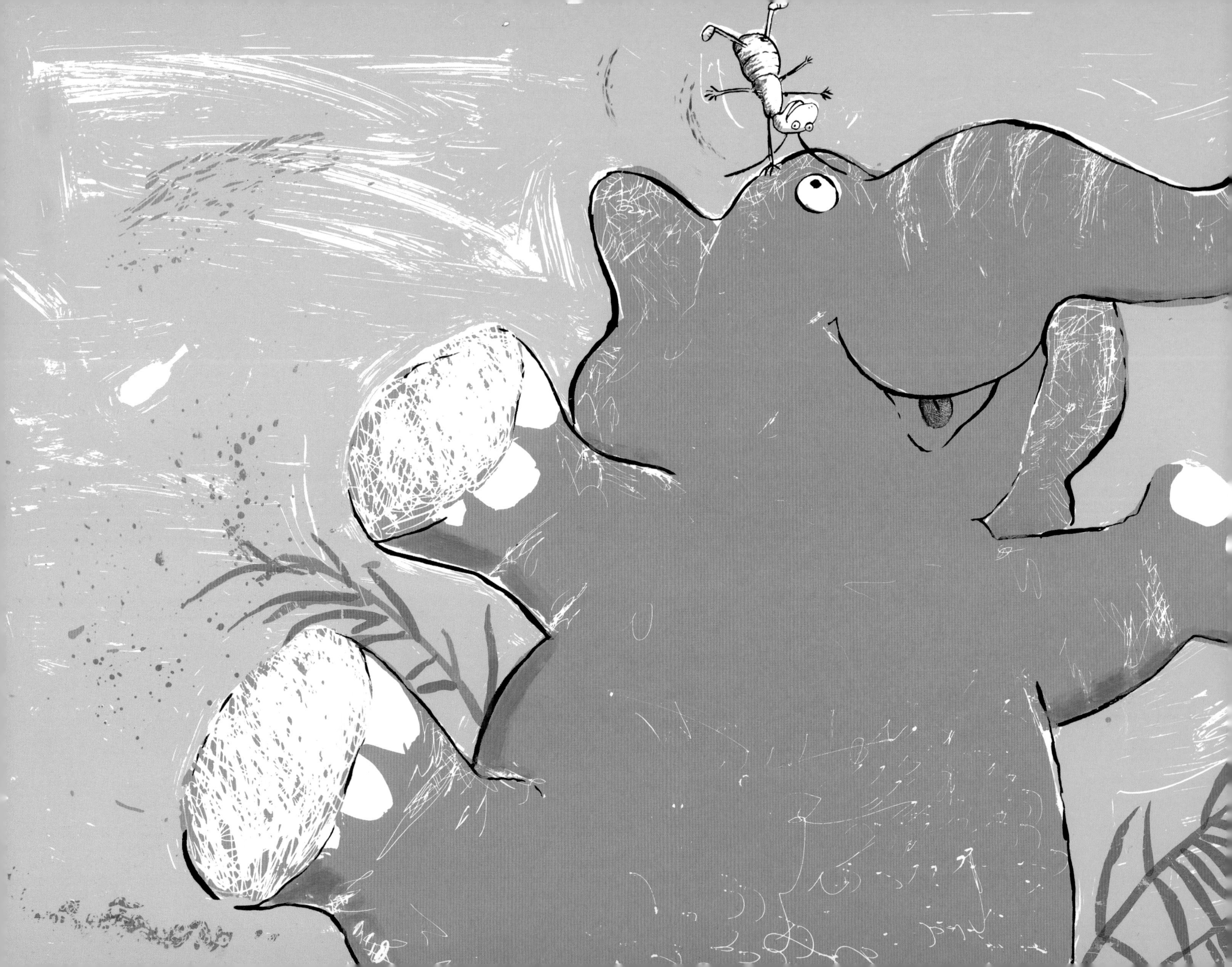

“Here!” cried the ant. “It ends right here! We’ve found the end of the ocean!”

“Hooray!” shouted the elephant, and he climbed back down the palm tree.

But on the way down, the little ant began to think some more.

"I'm glad to know where the ocean ends," he told the elephant, "but now I'm wondering, where does the ocean begin?"

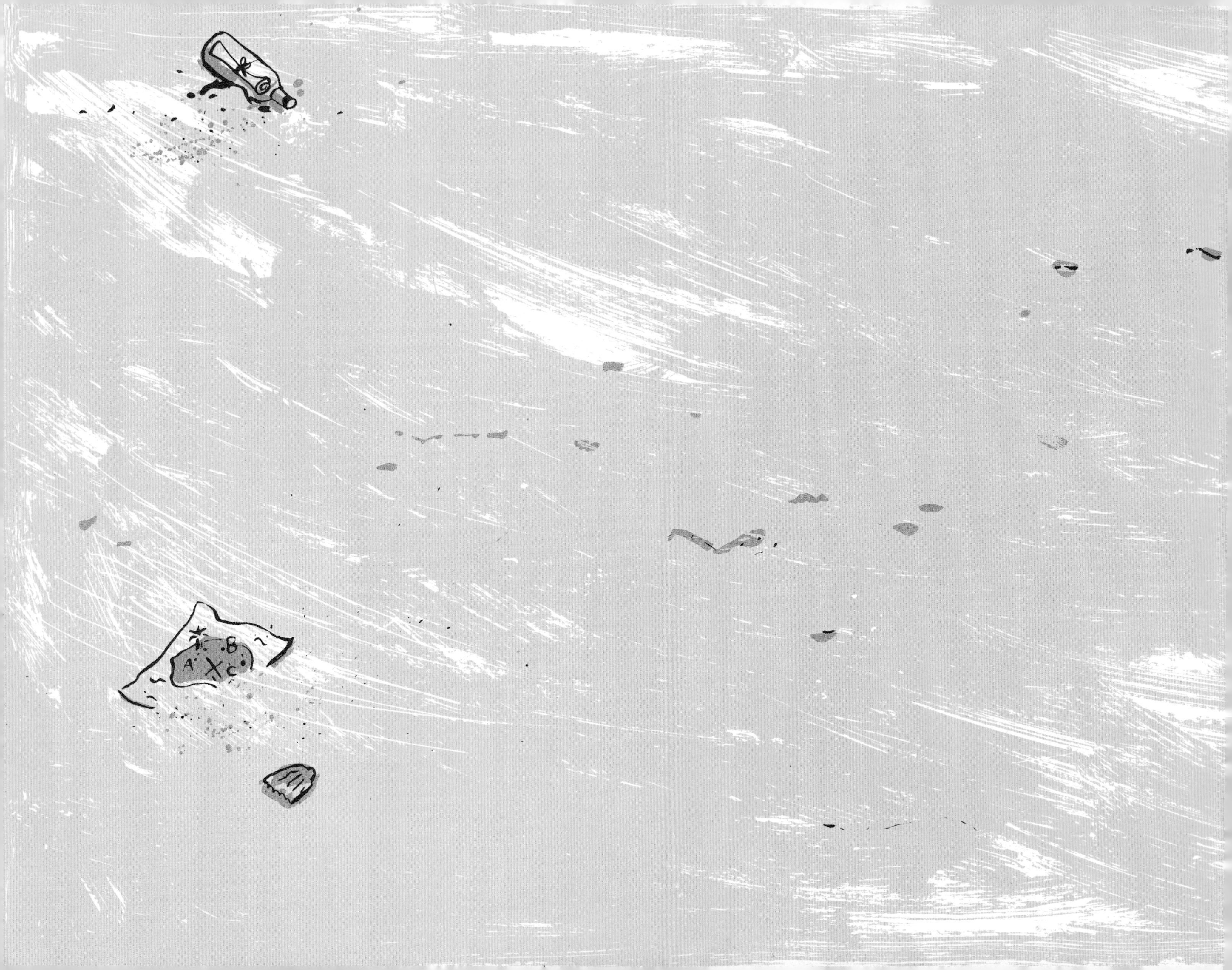
B
A
C